The
NUTCRACKER

This book is a gift for

Eliza Jane

from

Maw-Maw

2008

The NUTCRACKER

Retold by Norma Elizabeth

Illustrated by Anita S. Bice

Text copyright 1997 by Crane Hill Publishers
Illustrations copyright 1997 by Anita S. Bice

Printed in China
Published by Sweetwater Press, Birmingham, Alabama

Book design by Alice Pederson

Library of Congress Cataloging-in-Publication Data

Norma Elizabeth.
The Nutcracker / retold by Norma Elizabeth; illustrated by Anita S. Bice.
p.   cm.
Summary: After receiving a toy nutcracker as a Christmas gift from her godfa-
ther, a little girl helps break the spell and changes him into a
handsome prince.
ISBN 1-889372-56-0
[1. Fairy tales.] I. Bice, Anita S., ill. II. Title.
PZ8.N7535Nu 1997
[E]—DC21   97-29778
                   CIP
                   AC

The Nutcracker

Dedication

For Jeffrey,

Rebecca, and Brett,

with love, Norma

For Erin and Dana,

and with many thanks

to Carrie for her help,

with love, Anita

nce upon a time in Nuremberg, Germany, snowflakes fell softly on Christmas Eve, turning the whole city into a sparkling wonderland. In those days people had parties and gave gifts the night before Christmas instead of Christmas morning. All of the children tried to be on their best behavior, even though they were very excited. They couldn't wait for their grandparents and aunts and uncles and friends to arrive so they could open their presents.

Clara and her older brother Fritz waited for their guests in the parlor near the Christmas tree. They thought it was the most magnificent tree in the whole wide world. It reached almost to the ceiling, and every branch held a beautiful ornament that sparkled in the candlelight. A lovely angel with gossamer wings smiled down at them from the tip-top, and toys and packages tied with colorful bows peeked out from under the bottom branches.

The children impatiently watched their mother and father greet the people who came to their house. They wished everyone would hurry up and take off their hats and coats so the party could start!

lara and Fritz were delighted when Clara's godfather, Dr. Drosselmeir, arrived with an armful of presents. They knew his gifts would be the best of all because he was no ordinary doctor — he was an inventor. He created marvelous toys that could move and speak. That Christmas Eve Dr. Drosselmeir gave Fritz a lively jack-in-the-box and an army of splendid wooden soldiers. He gave Clara two windup dancing dolls, a miniature castle surrounded by a moat and beautiful gardens, and an elegantly carved, doll-size boat.

The children thanked Dr. Drosselmeir for the wonderful gifts and showed them to everyone at the party. But Dr. Drosselmeir had one more gift to give that night. Reaching deep inside the red lining of his purple cloak, he pulled out a long box tied with pink satin ribbon and placed it gently in Clara's arms.

Somehow Clara knew this was a very special gift, something her godfather had made just for her. She carefully untied the bow and opened the box. Inside she found a handsome wooden soldier in full-dress uniform. Clara thought to herself that the soldier's head was far too big for his body, and she wondered about his large jaws until Fritz exclaimed, "It's a nutcracker!" Clara put a small nut in the soldier's mouth and pressed the lever at the back of his head. The soldier easily cracked the nut and dropped it into Clara's hand.

"I want it!" yelled Fritz, yanking the nutcracker out of Clara's hand. He quickly stuffed several large nuts into the soldier's mouth and pressed down hard on the lever. With a painful crack, the soldier's jaws broke, and three of his perfectly formed teeth fell out.

"Oh, no!" cried Clara, reaching for the broken soldier and cradling him in her arms. The soldier's bright blue eyes seemed to look deep into hers, and Clara snuggled him tighter. Dr. Drosselmeir stooped over, picked up the soldier's broken teeth, and tucked them into one of the small pockets of his gold vest. Then he knelt down next to Clara and helped her wrap a handkerchief around the nutcracker's head to hold his broken jaws together.

Clara gently kissed the wounded soldier on the cheek, being careful not to disturb the bandage. She whispered that she loved him and would not let anyone hurt him ever again.

y this time it was almost midnight, and Dr. Drosselmeir and the other guests wished Fritz, Clara, and their parents a Merry Christmas and went home. Clara's mother helped her put on her nightgown, tucked her into her bed, and kissed her good night. As soon as her mother left her bedroom, Clara climbed out of bed and slipped quietly into the parlor — she wanted to make sure her nutcracker was safe for the night.

She gently tucked the wounded soldier into a doll-size bed in the glass cabinet where she and Fritz kept the wonderful toys Dr. Drosselmeir had made for them. She gave her beloved nutcracker another soft kiss on the cheek before she closed the cabinet door.

Clara suddenly felt so tired that she lay down on the sofa next to the cabinet and promptly fell fast asleep.

strange scratching sound woke her up, and when Clara opened her eyes, she let out a scream. Hundreds of mice were skittering across the room. Their leader, a mouse as big as Clara, was urging them toward the glass cabinet to attack the wooden soldiers Dr. Drosselmeir had made for Fritz. Clara's wounded nutcracker, riding a spirited horse Dr. Drosselmeir had also made, was leading the soldiers in the battle against the mice.

Clara started cheering on her beloved nutcracker and the wooden soldiers. They fought valiantly, but the mice outnumbered them. As Clara watched, her brave nutcracker courageously raised his sword, ready to attack the Mouse King.

eeing the danger her wounded soldier faced,
Clara sprang into action. She pulled off her
right slipper and threw it at the Mouse King,
shouting, "Leave my nutcracker alone!"

Clara's slipper hit the Mouse King and knocked off
his crown. Poof — the king and all his mice vanished!
Clara couldn't believe her eyes when the nutcracker's wounds
healed instantly and he turned into a handsome prince.

y dear Clara," he said, "you have saved my life!" The prince picked up the Mouse King's crown and offered it to Clara. "Please let me put this crown on your head and take you to my kingdom, the land of the *Sugar Plum Fairy*."

"Oh, yes," said Clara. "I'd like to see your kingdom."

aking Clara's hand, the prince led her to a pink lemonade stream that had appeared out of nowhere and helped her into a beautifully carved boat. As the prince guided the boat downstream, he told Clara about the spell a witch had cast on him when he was a little boy. The witch turned him into a nutcracker and told him that the only way he could become a prince again was to win a battle and have a beautiful lady fall in love with him. "Thank you, Clara, for loving me and helping me defeat the Mouse King and his mice," said the prince.

"You are most welcome," replied Clara, smiling happily.

As they rounded a bend in the stream, a beautiful castle came into view. "That is my home, Clara. The Sugar Plum Fairy will be waiting to greet us," the prince told her.

Clara clapped her hands in delight when their boat reached the stairs leading up from the moat to the castle. Gumdrops and meringue swirls lined the staircase that led through gardens of bright, colorful flowers and groves of red licorice shrubs and peppermint stick trees.

Just as the prince had told her, the Sugar Plum Fairy was waiting for them. She stood with her arms open, ready to hug them. Clara thought she was the most beautiful lady she had ever seen.

 he *Sugar* *Plum* *Fairy* led them
to the ballroom where people
from all over the kingdom had
gathered for a grand party to celebrate
the prince's homecoming and to honor Clara.

Clara and the prince sat together on a golden
throne and munched on delicious cookies and
candies while his loyal subjects entertained them
with music and dancing. Some of the dancers
twirled so fast that their feet hardly seemed to
touch the floor, and some of them leaped so
high that they seemed to touch the ceiling!

lara turned to the prince and said, "I wish I could dance like that!" Before the words were out of her mouth, Clara found herself in the midst of the dancers. She seemed to be dancing on air as she twirled faster and faster and leaped higher and higher. The prince joined her, and they danced until dawn.

s dawn cast its rosy tint across the morning sky and the birds began to sing, the prince helped Clara back into the beautifully carved boat and took her home.

"Thank you for a wonderful time," Clara told him when he leaned over and kissed her hand. She kept waving good-bye until his boat disappeared around the bend in the stream. Then she climbed into her bed, snuggled down under the blankets, and fell sound asleep.

A man's voice saying, "Merry Christmas!" woke her up. Then she heard her mother reply, "Merry Christmas, Dr. Drosselmeir!"

Clara sat up in bed — her godfather had arrived to eat Christmas breakfast with them. She couldn't wait to tell him about the Mouse King and the battle and her wounded nutcracker turning into a handsome prince — and the wonderful party in the Land of the Sugar Plum Fairy. She wanted to thank him again for his very special gift, the splendid nutcracker he had made just for her.

The End